Busy Busy Moose

Nancy Van Laan
Illustrated by Amy Rusch

 Houghton Mifflin Company Boston 2003

For my sweet second grandson, Sky,
who will one day read this book all by himself.
—N. V. L.

For Leopold and Daisy,
who keep me a busy busy mom. I love you.
—A. R.

Text copyright © 2003 by Nancy Van Laan
Illustrations copyright © 2003 by Amy Rusch

www.houghtonmifflinbooks.com

The text of this book is set in 15-point New Century Schoolbook.
The illustrations are ink and colored pencil.

Library of Congress Cataloging-in-Publication Data
Van Laan, Nancy.
Busy busy moose / by Nancy Van Laan ; illustrated by Amy Rusch.
p.   cm.
Summary: Moose helps his little animal friends in many
ways during the four seasons.
ISBN 0-395-96091-6
[1. Moose — Fiction. 2. Animals — Fiction. 3. Seasons — Fiction.]
I. Rusch, Amy, ill. II. Title.
PZ7.V3269 Bu   2001   [E] — dc21   00-027145

Manufactured in Singapore
TWP 10 9 8 7 6 5 4 3 2 1

Contents

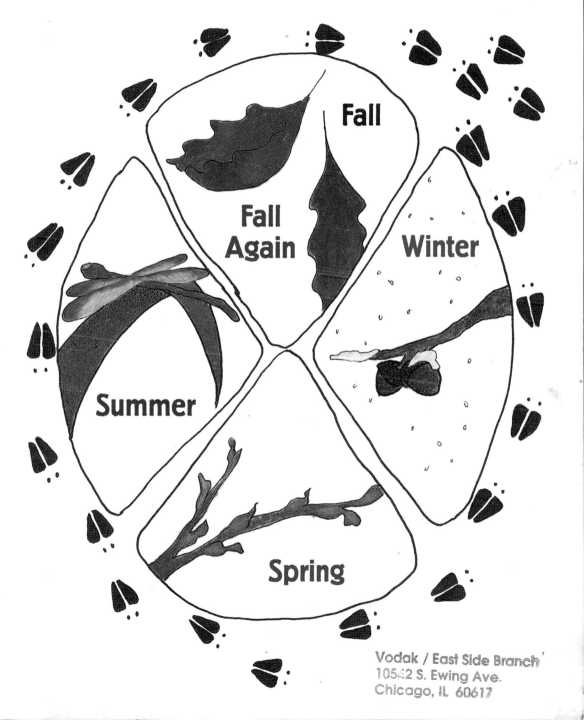

Fall

Fall
Again

Winter

Summer

Spring

Fall

There was a chill in the air.

Moose could see his breath.

He looked up.

The leaves were gold and red and brown.

"It must be fall," said Moose.

"I will go tell Beaver."

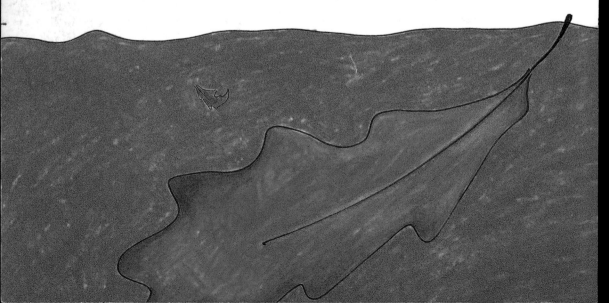

Moose did not need a house.
He did not need to gather acorns
or bark and twigs.
He did not need to gather anything at all.
Moose had nothing busy to do.

He walked into the middle
of a great wide field.
There he stood for a long time,
all alone.

Moose went to see Rabbit.

Rabbit also knew it was fall.

He was busy, too.

He was busy gathering bark and twigs.

Moose went to see Squirrel.

"Hello, Squirrel," said Moose.

"Do you know what season it is?"

"It is fall," said Squirrel.

"I can see my breath."

"Me, too!" said Moose.

"This is my busiest time of the year,"
said Squirrel. "I have to hide acorns."

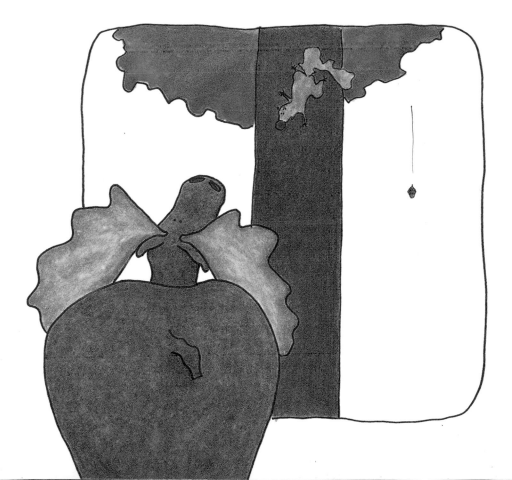

"Hello, Beaver," said Moose.

"Do you know what season it is?"

"Yes," said Beaver. "It is fall."

"How did you guess?" asked Moose.

"I can see my breath," said Beaver.

"The leaves are gold and red and brown."

"Oh," said Moose. "We both saw
the same things."

"And," said Beaver,

"this is the busiest time of the year."

"Why?" asked Moose.

"I have to make my winter house,"
said Beaver.

One tiny bird landed on Moose's antler.

Then another.

And another.

A flock of birds flew by.

They were on their way south for the winter.

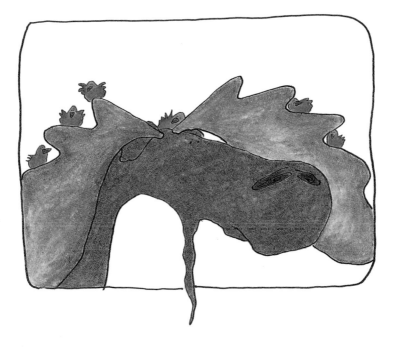

Soon Moose's antlers were full of birds.
He did not know they were there.

Rabbit hopped by.

"You look very busy," he said.

"Busy?" said Moose.

"Busy doing what?"

"Busy being a tree," said Rabbit.

"Your antlers are full of birds."

Moose looked surprised.

"You are a perfect resting spot,"
said Rabbit, and he hopped off.

Oh, thought Moose.

I must stand very still.

This will be my job.

Each day Moose stood in the field.
Each day a new flock of birds flew by.
Each day his antlers were full of birds.
Now fall was the busiest time
of the year for Moose, too.

Winter

"Halloo, Moose!" Beaver called.

"Come see my new winter home!"

Moose waded all the way
to the other side of the pond.
He stuck his big nose through the
small front door.
"What a fine home," said Moose.
"Please don't come in," said Beaver.
"You are too big."

"HALLOOOO!"

It was Rabbit.

He was on the other side of the pond.

"Come see my new home," called Beaver.

But the water was too deep.

Moose waded over to Rabbit.

"Hop on," said Moose.

Moose took Rabbit across the deep pond.

"Come in, Rabbit," said Beaver.

"Your home is so warm and dry," said Rabbit.

Moose poked his big wet nose inside.

"Hmmm," said Moose.

"HALLOOOO!"

It was Squirrel.

"Come see my new home," said Beaver.

But the water was too deep.

"Here I come," said Moose.

"You are a perfect ferry boat," said Squirrel.

"Come in," said Beaver to Squirrel.
"Your home is just the right size,"
said Squirrel.
Moose poked his big nose inside.
Hmmm, thought Moose.

"HALLOOOO!" said Mouse.
So Moose carried Mouse to Beaver's
new home, too.

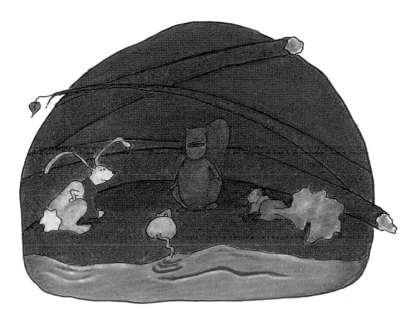

Beaver, Rabbit, Squirrel, and Mouse
sat inside, warm and dry.
Only Moose's nose was warm and dry.
The rest of him was not.

It was time to say goodbye.

"Please come again soon," said Beaver.

"We shall!" said Rabbit, Squirrel, and Mouse.

They hopped onto Moose.

Back across the pond they went.

Beaver watched Moose cross the pond again.

Poor Moose!

How weary he must be.

That month, Beaver had lots of visitors.

Each day, Moose was a ferry boat.

He was tired of this job.

But he did not quit.

One bitterly cold day, the pond froze.
No water. Just thick ice.
"Hooray!" said Moose.

Now Rabbit, Squirrel, and Mouse
hopped across—
all by themselves.
And Moose could rest.

Spring

It was spring.
The birds were nesting.
It was their busiest time of the year.
Moose was busy being himself.

One day while Moose was napping,
a baby bird fell out of its nest.

Guess where it landed?

The mama bird flew round and round.

She fussed and fussed.

Moose woke up.

He thought she was admiring
his new antlers.

Along came Beaver.

"You have a houseguest," said Beaver.

"I do?" said Moose.

Moose walked to the pond.

He looked at his reflection.

"Oh, my!" said Moose.

"Last fall I was the perfect resting spot."

"Now," said Beaver, "you are a perfect
nesting spot."

But when Moose tried to walk again,
the mama bird flew round his head.
She fussed and fussed.
She screeched in his ear:
Trees don't walk!

Moose tipped his head
to the right.
The baby bird hopped to
his right antler.

He tipped his head
to the left.
The baby bird hopped to
his left antler.

He tipped his head all the way back.
The baby bird landed on his nose.

That tickled Moose.

"AHHHHHHH-CHOOOOOO!"

Away went the baby bird.

He could fly!

"Now you can just be Moose again," said Beaver.
"Good," said Moose. "In the spring,
being just a moose is what I do best."

Summer

It was a hot summer day.

Moose was grazing in the meadow.

He did not look busy.

But he was.

Moose was busy thinking:

Summer is a time for thinking good thoughts.

It is a time to dream.

A time to plan.

Beaver was floating in his pond.

He did not look busy.

But he was.

Beaver was busy thinking:

Summer is a time for thinking good thoughts.

It is a time to dream.

A time to plan.

Moose dreamed of winter.

He saw himself busy being a ferry boat.

Beaver dreamed of winter, too.

He saw himself in his warm, dry house.

Suddenly, Beaver had an idea.

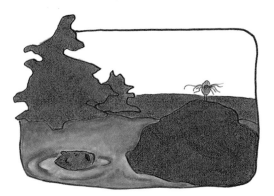

Moose had an idea, too.

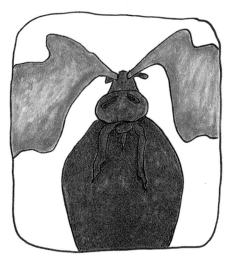

That night, while Beaver slept,
Moose got busy.
He rolled rocks, lots of big rocks,
down to the creek.

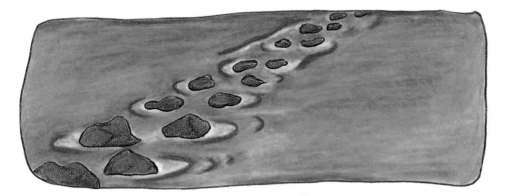

The next day, while Moose
was in the meadow,
Beaver got busy.
He swam back and forth,
his mouth full of sticks.

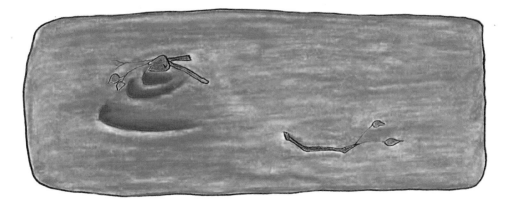

At the end of the day Moose went to see Beaver.
They always spent the end of each day together.
They liked to take turns talking.
Today Moose went first.
"I have a surprise for you, Beaver."
"Oh," said Beaver.
"I have a surprise for you, too."
"Follow me," said Moose.
"You can *walk* on my surprise."
Moose crossed the creek on the rocks.
So did Beaver.
"Now," said Moose, "you can
have visitors all winter long!"

Then Moose snorted.
"Beaver, where is your house?"
"Oh, Moose!" said Beaver.
"That was *my* surprise for *you*!"
Beaver pointed. His new home was
now on the other side of the pond.
Moose and Beaver laughed and laughed.

Beaver hopped on Moose's back.

Together they went to see

Beaver's new winter home.

This time, it was large enough to fit

half a moose inside.

Fall Again

There was a chill in the air.
Moose could see his breath.
He looked up.
The leaves were gold and red and brown.
"Hooray!" said Moose.
"It's fall again."

He walked into the middle
of the great wide field . . .

...and waited.